The Velvet Glove

The Velvet Glove

Harry Harrison

ÆGYPAN PRESS

This novel first appeared in the November, 1956, issue of *Fantastic Universe.*

Harry Harrison was also known by the name Henry Maxwell Dempsey.

Special thanks to Greg Weeks, Stephen Blundell, and the On-line Distributed Proofreading Team (which can be found at http://www.pgdp.net).

The Velvet Glove
A publication of
ÆGYPAN PRESS

www.aegypan.com

SF writer and editor Harry Harrison explores a not too distant future where robots — particularly specialist robots who don't know their place — have quite a rough time of it. True, the Robot Equality Act had been passed — but so what?

New York was a bad town for robots that year. In fact, all over the country it was bad for robots. . . .

*J*on Venex fitted the key into the hotel room door. He had asked for a large room, the largest in the hotel, and paid the desk clerk extra for it. All he could do now was pray that he hadn't been cheated. He didn't dare complain or try to get his money back. He heaved a sigh of relief as the door swung open, it was bigger than he had expected — fully three feet wide by five feet long. There was more than enough room to work in. He would have his leg off in a jiffy and by morning his limp would be gone.

There was the usual adjustable hook on the back wall. He slipped it through the recessed ring in the back of his neck and kicked himself up until his feet hung free of the floor. His legs relaxed with a rattle as he cut off all power from his waist down.

The overworked leg motor would have to cool down before he could work on it, plenty of time to skim through the newspaper. With the chronic worry of the unemployed, he snapped it open at the want-ads and ran his eye down the *Help Wanted – Robot* column. There was nothing for him under the Specialist heading, even the Unskilled Labor listings were bare and unpromising. New York was a bad town for robots this year.

The want-ads were just as depressing as usual but he could always get a lift from the comic section. He even had a favorite strip, a fact that he scarcely dared mention to himself. "Rattly Robot," a dull-witted mechanical clod who was continually falling over himself and getting into trouble. It was a repellent caricature, but could still be very funny. Jon was just starting to read it when the ceiling light went out.

It was ten P.M., curfew hour for robots. Lights out and lock yourself in until six in the morning, eight hours of boredom and darkness for all except the few night workers. But there were ways of getting around the letter of a law that didn't concern itself with a definition of visible light. Sliding aside some of the shielding around his atomic generator, Jon turned up the gain. As it began to run a little hot the heat waves streamed out — visible to him as infra-red rays. He finished reading the paper in the warm, clear light of his abdomen.

The thermocouple in the tip of his second finger left hand, he tested the temperature of his leg. It was soon cool enough to work on. The waterproof gasket stripped off easily, exposing the power leads, nerve wires and the weakened knee joint. The wires disconnected, Jon unscrewed the knee above the joint and carefully placed it on the shelf in front of him. With loving care he took the replacement part from his hip pouch. It was the product of toil, purchased with his savings from three months employment on the Jersey pig farm.

Jon was standing on one leg testing the new knee joint when the ceiling fluorescent flickered and came back on. Five-thirty already, he had just finished in time. A shot of oil on the new bearing completed the

job; he stowed away the tools in the pouch and un-
locked the door.

The unused elevator shaft acted as waste chute, he
slipped his newspaper through a slot in the door as he
went by. Keeping close to the wall, he picked his way
carefully down the grease-stained stairs. He slowed his
pace at the 17th floor as two other mechs turned in
ahead of him. They were obviously butchers or meat-
cutters; where the right hand should have been on each
of them there stuck out a wicked, foot-long knife. As
they approached the foot of the stairs they stopped to
slip the knives into the plastic sheaths that were bolted
to their chestplates. Jon followed them down the ramp
into the lobby.

The room was filled to capacity with robots of all
sizes, forms and colors. Jon Venex's greater height
enabled him to see over their heads to the glass doors
that opened onto the street. It had rained the night
before and the rising sun drove red glints from the
puddles on the sidewalk. Three robots, painted snow
white to show they were night workers, pushed the
doors open and came in. No one went out as the curfew
hadn't ended yet. They milled around slowly talking
in low voices.

The only human being in the entire lobby was the
night clerk dozing behind the counter. The clock over
his head said five minutes to six. Shifting his glance
from the clock, Jon became aware of a squat black
robot waving to attract his attention. The powerful
arms and compact build identified him as a member
of the Diger family, one of the most numerous groups.
He pushed through the crowd and clapped Jon on the
back with a resounding clang.

"Jon Venex! I knew it was you as soon as I saw you
sticking up out of this crowd like a green tree trunk. I
haven't seen you since the old days on Venus!"

Jon didn't need to check the number stamped on
the short one's scratched chestplate. Alec Diger had
been his only close friend during those thirteen boring
years at Orange Sea Camp. A good chess player and a
whiz at Two-handed Handball, they had spent all their
off time together. They shook hands, with the extra
squeeze that means friendliness.

"Alec, you beat-up little grease pot, what brings you
to New York?"

"The burning desire to see something besides rain
and jungle, if you must know. After you bought out,
things got just too damn dull. I began working two
shifts a day in that foul diamond mine, and then three
a day for the last month to get enough credits to buy
my contract and passage back to earth. I was under-
ground so long that the photocell on my right eye
burned out when the sunlight hit it."

He leaned forward with a hoarse confidential whisper, "If you want to know the truth, I had a sixty-carat
diamond stuck behind the eye lens. I sold it here on
earth for two hundred credits, gave me six months of
easy living. It's all gone now, so I'm on my way to the
employment exchange." His voice boomed loud again,
"And how about *you?*"

Jon Venex chuckled at his friend's frank approach
to life. "It's just been the old routine with me, a run
of odd jobs until I got side-swiped by a bus — it
fractured my knee bearing. The only job I could get
with a bad leg was feeding slops to pigs. Earned enough
to fix the knee — and here *I* am."

Alec jerked his thumb at a rust-colored, three-foot-
tall robot that had come up quietly beside him. "If you
think you've got trouble take a look at Dik here, that's
no coat of paint on him. Dik Dryer, meet Jon Venex
an old buddy of mine."

Jon bent over to shake the little mech's hand. His eye shutters dilated as he realized what he had thought was a coat of paint was a thin layer of rust that coated Dik's metal body. Alec scratched a shiny path in the rust with his fingertip. His voice was suddenly serious.

"Dik was designed for operation in the Martian desert. It's as dry as a fossil bone there so his skinflint company cut corners on the stainless steel.

"When they went bankrupt he was sold to a firm here in the city. After a while the rust started to eat in and slow him down, they gave Dik his contract and threw him out."

The small robot spoke for the first time, his voice grated and scratched. "Nobody will hire me like this, but I can't get repaired until I get a job." His arms squeaked and grated as he moved them. "I'm going by the Robot Free Clinic again today, they said they might be able to do something."

Alec Diger rumbled in his deep chest. "Don't put too much faith in those people. They're great at giving out tenth-credit oil capsules or a little free wire — but don't depend on them for anything important."

It was six now, the robots were pushing through the doors into the silent streets. They joined the crowd moving out, Jon slowing his stride so his shorter friends could keep pace. Dik Dryer moved with a jerking, irregular motion, his voice as uneven as the motion of his body.

"Jon — Venex, I don't recognize your family name. Something to do — with Venus — perhaps."

"Venus is right, Venus Experimental — there are only twenty-two of us in the family. We have waterproof, pressure-resistant bodies for working down on the ocean bottom. The basic idea was all right, we did our part, only there wasn't enough money in the channel-dredging contract to keep us all working. I bought out my original contract at half price and became a free robot."

Dik vibrated his rusted diaphragm. "Being free isn't all it should be. I some — times wish the Robot Equality Act hadn't been passed. I would just l-love to be owned by a nice rich company with a machine shop and a — mountain of replacement parts."

"You don't really mean that, Dik," Alec Diger clamped a heavy black arm across his shoulders. "Things aren't perfect now, we know that, but it's certainly a lot better than the old days, we were just hunks of machinery then. Used twenty-four hours a day until we were worn out and then thrown in the junk pile. No thanks, I'll take my chances with things as they are."

*J*on and Alec turned into the employment exchange, saying good-bye to Dik who went on slowly down the street. They pushed up the crowded ramp and joined the line in front of the registration desk. The bulletin board next to the desk held a scattering of white slips announcing job openings. A clerk was pinning up new additions.

Venex scanned them with his eyes, stopping at one circled in red.

ROBOTS NEEDED IN THESE CATEGORIES. APPLY AT ONCE TO CHAINJET, LTD., 1219 BROADWAY.

Fasten
Flyer
Atommel
Filmer
Venex

Jon rapped excitedly on Alec Diger's neck. "Look there, a job in my own specialty — I can get my old pay rate! See you back at the hotel tonight — and good luck in your job hunting."

Alec waved good-bye. "Let's hope the job's as good as you think, I never trust those things until I have my credits in my hand."

Jon walked quickly from the employment exchange, his long legs eating up the blocks. *Good old Alec, he didn't believe in anything he couldn't touch. Perhaps he was right, but why try to be unhappy. The world wasn't too bad this morning — his leg worked fine, prospects of a good job — he hadn't felt this cheerful since the day he was activated.*

Turning the corner at a brisk pace he collided with a man coming from the opposite direction. Jon had stopped on the instant, but there wasn't time to jump aside. The obese individual jarred against him and fell to the ground. From the height of elation to the depths of despair in an instant — he had injured a *human being!*

He bent to help the man to his feet, but the other would have none of that. He evaded the friendly hand and screeched in a high-pitched voice.

"Officer, officer, police . . . HELP! I've been attacked — a mad robot . . . HELP!"

A crowd was gathering — staying at a respectful distance — but making an angry muttering noise. Jon stood motionless, his head reeling at the enormity of what he had done. A policeman pushed his way through the crowd.

"Seize him, officer, shoot him down . . . he struck me . . . almost killed me . . ." The man shook with rage, his words thickening to a senseless babble.

The policeman had his .75 recoilless revolver out and pressed against Jon's side.

"This *man* has charged you with a serious crime, *grease-can*. I'm taking you into the station house — to talk about it." He looked around nervously, waving his gun to open a path through the tightly packed crowd. They moved back grudgingly, with murmurs of disapproval.

Jon's thoughts swirled in tight circles. How did a catastrophe like this happen, where was it going to end? He didn't dare tell the truth, that would mean he was calling the man a liar. There had been six robots power-lined in the city since the first of the year. If he dared speak in his own defense there would be a jumper to the street lighting circuit and a seventh burned out hulk in the police morgue.

A feeling of resignation swept through him, there was no way out. If the man pressed charges it would mean a term of penal servitude, though it looked now as if he would never live to reach the court. The papers had been whipping up a lot of anti-robe feeling, you could feel it behind the angry voices, see it in the narrowed eyes and clenched fists. The crowd was slowly changing into a mob, a mindless mob as yet, but capable of turning on him at any moment.

"What's goin' on here. . . ?" It was a booming voice, with a quality that dragged at the attention of the crowd.

A giant cross-continent freighter was parked at the curb. The driver swung down from the cab and pushed his way through the people. The policeman shifted his gun as the man strode up to him.

"That's my robot you got there, Jack, don't put any holes in him!" He turned on the man who had been shouting accusations. "Fatty here, is the world's biggest liar. The robot was standing here waiting for me to park the truck. Fatty must be as blind as he is stupid, I saw the whole thing. He knocks himself down walking into the robe, then starts hollering for the cops."

The other man could take no more. His face crimson with anger he rushed toward the trucker, his fists swinging in ungainly circles. They never landed, the truck driver put a meaty hand on the other's face and seated him on the sidewalk for the second time.

The onlookers roared with laughter, the power-lining and the robot were forgotten. The fight was between two men now, the original cause had slipped from their minds. Even the policeman allowed himself a small smile as he holstered his gun and stepped forward to separate the men.

The trucker turned towards Jon with a scowl.

"Come on you aboard the truck – you've caused me enough trouble for one day. What a junkcan!"

The crowd chuckled as he pushed Jon ahead of him into the truck and slammed the door behind them. Jamming the starter with his thumb he gunned the thunderous diesels into life and pulled out into the traffic.

Jon moved his jaw, but there were no words to come out. Why had this total stranger helped him, what could he say to show his appreciation? He knew that all humans weren't robe-haters, why it was even rumored that some humans treated robots as *equals* instead of machines. The driver must be one of these mythical individuals, there was no other way to explain his actions.

Driving carefully with one hand the man reached up behind the dash and drew out a thin, plastikoid booklet. He handed it to Jon who quickly scanned the title, *Robot Slaves in a World Economy* by Philpott Asimov II.

"If you're caught reading that thing they'll execute you on the spot. Better stick it between the insulation on your generator, you can always burn it if you're picked up.

"Read it when you're alone, it's got a lot of things in it that you know nothing about. Robots aren't really inferior to humans, in fact they're superior in most things. There is even a little history in there to show that robots aren't the first ones to be treated as second class citizens. You may find it a little hard to believe, but human beings once treated each other just the way they treat robots now. That's one of the reasons I'm active in this movement — sort of like the fellow who was burned helping others stay away from the fire."

He smiled a warm, friendly smile in Jon's direction, the whiteness of his teeth standing out against the rich ebony brown of his features.

"I'm heading towards US-1, can I drop you any-wheres on the way?"

"The Chainjet Building please — I'm applying for a job."

They rode the rest of the way in silence. Before he opened the door the driver shook hands with Jon.

"Sorry about calling you *junkcan,* but the crowd expected it." He didn't look back as he drove away.

Jon had to wait a half hour for his turn, but the receptionist finally signalled him towards the door of the interviewer's room. He stepped in quickly and turned to face the man seated at the transplastic desk, an upset little man with permanent worry wrinkles stamped in his forehead. The little man shoved the papers on the desk around angrily, occasionally mak-ing crabbed little notes on the margins. He flashed a birdlike glance up at Jon.

"Yes, yes, be quick. What is it you want?"

"You posted a help wanted notice, I —"

The man cut him off with a wave of his hand. "All right let me see your ID tag . . . quickly, there are others waiting."

Jon thumbed the tag out of his waist slot and handed it across the desk. The interviewer read the code number, then began running his finger down a long list of similar figures. He stopped suddenly and looked sideways at Jon from under his lowered lids.

"You have made a mistake, we have no opening for you."

Jon began to explain to the man that the notice had requested his specialty, but he was waved to silence. As the interviewer handed back the tag he slipped a card out from under the desk blotter and held it in front of Jon's eyes. He held it there for only an instant, knowing that the written message was recorded instantly by the robot's photographic vision and eidetic memory. The card dropped into the ash tray and flared into embers at the touch of the man's pencil-heater.

Jon stuffed the ID tag back into the slot and read over the message on the card as he walked down the stairs to the street. There were six lines of typewritten copy with no signature.

To Venex Robot: You are urgently needed on a top secret company project. There are suspected informers in the main office, so you are being hired in this unusual manner. Go at once to 787 Washington Street and ask for Mr. Coleman.

Jon felt an immense sensation of relief. For a moment there, he was sure the job had been a false lead. He saw nothing unusual in the method of hiring. The big corporations were immensely jealous of their research discoveries and went to great lengths to keep them secret — at the same time resorting to any means to ferret out their business rivals' secrets. There might still be a chance to get this job.

*T*he burly bulk of a lifter was moving back and forth in the gloom of the ancient warehouse stacking crates in ceiling-high rows. Jon called to him, the robot swung up his forklift and rolled over on noiseless tires. When Jon questioned him he indicated a stairwell against the rear wall.

"Mr. Coleman's office is down in back, the door is marked." The lifter put his fingertips against Jon's ear pick-ups and lowered his voice to the merest shadow of a whisper. It would have been inaudible to human ears, but Jon could hear him easily, the sounds being carried through the metal of the other's body.

"He's the meanest man you ever met — he hates robots so be *ever* so polite. If you can use 'sir' five times in one sentence you're perfectly safe."

Jon swept the shutter over one eye tube in a conspiratorial wink, the large mech did the same as he rolled away. Jon turned and went down the dusty stairwell and knocked gently on Mr. Coleman's door.

Coleman was a plump little individual in a conservative purple-and-yellow business suit. He kept glancing from Jon to the Robot General Catalog checking the Venex specifications listed there. Seemingly satisfied he slammed the book shut.

"Gimme your tag and back against that wall to get measured."

Jon laid his ID tag on the desk and stepped towards the wall. "Yes, sir, here it is, sir." Two "sir" on that one, not bad for the first sentence. He wondered idly if he could put five of them in one sentence without the man knowing he was being made a fool of.

He became aware of the danger an instant too late. The current surged through the powerful electromagnet behind the plaster flattening his metal body helplessly against the wall. Coleman was almost dancing with glee.

"We got him, Druce, he's mashed flatter than a stinking tin-can on a rock, can't move a motor. Bring that junk in here and let's get him ready."

Druce had a mechanic's coveralls on over his street suit and a tool box slung under one arm. He carried a little black metal can at arm's length, trying to get as far from it as possible. Coleman shouted at him with annoyance.

"That bomb can't go off until it's armed, stop acting like a child. Put it on that grease-can's leg and *quick!*"

Grumbling under his breath, Druce spot-welded the metal flanges of the bomb onto Jon's leg a few inches above his knee. Coleman tugged at it to be certain it was secure, then twisted a knob in the side and pulled out a glistening length of pin. There was a cold little click from inside the mechanism as it armed itself.

Jon could do nothing except watch, even his vocal diaphragm was locked by the magnetic field. He had more than a suspicion however that he was involved in something other than a "secret business deal." He cursed his own stupidity for walking blindly into the situation.

The magnetic field cut off and he instantly raced his extensor motors to leap forward. Coleman took a plastic box out of his pocket and held his thumb over a switch inset into its top.

"Don't make any quick moves, junk-yard, this little transmitter is keyed to a receiver in that bomb on your leg. One touch of my thumb, up you go in a cloud of smoke and come down in a shower of nuts and bolts." He signalled to Druce who opened a closet door. "And in case you want to be heroic, just think of him."

Coleman jerked his thumb at the sodden shape on the floor; a filthily attired man of indistinguishable age whose only interesting feature was the black bomb strapped tightly across his chest. He peered unseeingly from red-rimmed eyes and raised the almost empty whiskey bottle to his mouth. Coleman kicked the door shut.

"He's just some Bowery bum we dragged in, Venex, but that doesn't make any difference to you, does it? He's human — and a robot can't kill *anybody!* That rummy has a bomb on him tuned to the same frequency as yours, if you don't play ball with us he gets a two-foot hole blown in his chest."

Coleman was right, Jon didn't dare make any false moves. All of his early mental training as well as Circuit 92 sealed inside his brain case would prevent him from harming a human being. He felt trapped, caught by these people for some unknown purpose.

Coleman had pushed back a tarpaulin to disclose a ragged hole in the concrete floor, the opening extended into the earth below. He waved Jon over.

"The tunnel is in good shape for about thirty feet, then you'll find a fall. Clean all the rock and dirt out until you break through into the storm sewer, then come back. And you better be alone. If you tip the cops both you and the old stew go out together — now move."

The shaft had been dug recently and shored with packing crates from the warehouse overhead. It ended abruptly in a wall of fresh sand and stone. Jon began shoveling it into the little wheelbarrow they had given him.

He had emptied four barrow loads and was filling the fifth when he uncovered the hand, a robot's hand made of green metal. He turned his headlight power up and examined the hand closely, there could be no doubt about it. These gaskets on the joints, the rivet pattern at the base of the thumb meant only one thing, it was the dismembered hand of a Venex robot.

Quickly, yet gently, he shoveled away the rubble behind the hand and unearthed the rest of the robot. The torso was crushed and the power circuits shorted, battery acid was dripping from an ugly rent in the side. With infinite care Jon snapped the few remaining wires that joined the neck to the body and laid the green head on the barrow. It stared at him like a skull, the shutters completely dilated, but no glow of life from the tubes behind them.

He was scraping the mud from the number on the battered chestplate when Druce lowered himself into the tunnel and flashed the brilliant beam of a hand-spot down its length.

"Stop playing with that junk and get digging — or you'll end up the same as him. This tunnel has gotta be through by tonight."

Jon put the dismembered parts on the barrow with the sand and rock and pushed the whole load back up the tunnel, his thoughts running in unhappy circles. A dead robot was a terrible thing, and one of his family too. But there was something wrong about this robot, something that was quite inexplicable, the number on the plate had been "17," yet he remembered only too well the day that a water-shorted motor had killed Venex 17 in the Orange Sea.

It took Jon four hours to drive the tunnel as far as the ancient granite wall of the storm sewer. Druce gave him a short pinch bar and he levered out enough of the big blocks to make a hole large enough to let him through into the sewer.

When he climbed back into the office he tried to look casual as he dropped the pinch bar to the floor by his feet and seated himself on the pile of rubble in the corner. He moved around to make a comfortable seat for himself and his fingers grabbed the severed neck of Venex 17.

Coleman swiveled around in his chair and squinted at the wall clock. He checked the time against his tie-pin watch, with a grunt of satisfaction he turned back and stabbed a finger at Jon.

"Listen, you green junk-pile, at 1900 hours you're going to do a job, and there aren't going to be any slip ups. You go down that sewer and into the Hudson River. The outlet is under water, so you won't be seen from the docks. Climb down to the bottom and walk 200 yards north, that should put you just under a ship. Keep your eyes open, *but don't show any lights!* About halfway down the keel of the ship you'll find a chain hanging.

"Climb the chain, pull loose the box that's fastened to the hull at the top and bring it back here. No mistakes — or you know what happens."

Jon nodded his head. His busy fingers had been separating the wires in the amputated neck. When they had been straightened and put into a row he memorized their order with one flashing glance.

He ran over the color code in his mind and compared it with the memorized leads. The twelfth wire was the main cranial power lead, number six was the return wire.

With his precise touch he separated these two from the pack and glanced idly around the room. Druce was dozing on a chair in the opposite corner. Coleman was talking on the phone, his voice occasionally rising in a petulant whine. This wasn't interfering with his attention to Jon — and the radio switch still held tightly in left hand.

Jon's body blocked Coleman's vision, as long as Druce stayed asleep he would be able to work on the head unobserved. He activated a relay in his forearm and there was a click as the waterproof cover on an exterior socket swung open. This was a power outlet from his battery that was used to operate motorized tools and lights underwater.

If Venex 17's head had been severed for less than three weeks he could reactivate it. Every robot had a small storage battery inside his skull, if the power to the brain was cut off the battery would provide the minimum standby current to keep the brain alive. The robe would be unconscious until full power was restored.

Jon plugged the wires into his arm-outlet and slowly raised the current to operating level. There was a tense moment of waiting, then 17's eye shutters suddenly closed. When they opened again the eye tubes were glowing warmly. They swept the room with one glance then focused on Jon.

The right shutter clicked shut while the other began opening and closing in rapid fashion. It was International code — being sent as fast as the solenoid could be operated. Jon concentrated on the message.

Telephone — call emergency operator — tell her "signal 14" help will —

The shutter stopped in the middle of a code group, the light of reason dying from the eyes.

For one instant Jon's heart leaped in panic, until he realized that 17 had deliberately cut the power. Druce's harsh voice rasped in his ear.

"What you doing with that? None of your funny robot tricks. I know your kind, plotting all kinds of things in them tin domes." His voice trailed off into a stream of incomprehensible profanity. With sudden spite he lashed his foot out and sent 17's head crashing against the wall.

The dented, green head rolled to a stop at Jon's feet, the face staring up at him in mute agony. It was only

Circuit 92 that prevented him from injuring a *human*.
As his motors revved up to send him hurtling forward
the control relays clicked open. He sank against the
debris, paralyzed for the instant. As soon as the rush
of anger was gone he would regain control of his body.

They stood as if frozen in a tableau. The robot
slumped backward, the man leaning forward, his face
twisted with unreasoning hatred. The head lay between
them like a symbol of death.

Coleman's voice cut through the air of tenseness like
a knife.

"*Druce*, stop playing with the grease-can and get
down to the main door to let Little Willy and his
junk-brokers in. You can have it all to yourself after-
ward."

The angry man turned reluctantly, but pushed out
of the door at Coleman's annoyed growl. Jon sat down
against the wall, his mind sorting out the few facts with
lightning precision. There was no room in his thoughts
for Druce, the man had become just one more factor
in a complex problem.

Call the emergency operator — that meant this was
no local matter, responsible authorities must be involved. Only the government could be behind a thing
as major as this. Signal 14 — that inferred a complex
set of arrangements, forces that could swing into action
at a moment's notice. There was no indication where
this might lead, but the only thing to do was to get out
of here and make that phone call. And quick. Druce
was bringing in more people, junk-brokers, whatever
they were. Any action that he took would have to be
done before they returned.

Even as Jon followed this train of logic his fingers
were busy. Palming a wrench, he was swiftly loosening
the main retaining nut on his hip joint. It dropped free
in his hand, only the pivot pin remained now to hold

his leg on. He climbed slowly to his feet and moved towards Coleman's desk.

"Mr. Coleman, sir, it's time to go down to the ship now, should I leave now, sir?"

Jon spoke the words slowly as he walked forward, apparently going to the door, but angling at the same time towards the plump man's desk.

"You got thirty minutes yet, go sit — *say*. . .!"

The words were cut off. Fast as a human reflex is, it is the barest crawl compared to the lightning action of electronic reflex. At the instant Coleman was first aware of Jon's motion, the robot had finished his leap and lay sprawled across the desk, his leg off at the hip and clutched in his hand.

"YOU'LL KILL YOURSELF IF YOU TOUCH THE BUTTON!"

The words were part of the calculated plan. Jon bellowed them in the startled man's ear as he stuffed the dismembered leg down the front of the man's baggy slacks. It had the desired effect, Coleman's finger stabbed at the button but stopped before it made contact. He stared down with bulging eyes at the little black box of death peeping out of his waistband.

Jon hadn't waited for the reaction. He pushed backward from the desk and stopped to grab the stolen pinch bar off the floor. A mighty one-legged leap brought him to the locked closet; he stabbed the bar into the space between the door and frame and heaved.

Coleman was just starting to struggle the bomb out of his pants when the action was over. The closet open, Jon seized the heavy strap holding the second bomb on the rummy's chest and snapped it like a thread. He threw the bomb into Coleman's corner, giving the man one more thing to worry about. It had cost him a leg, but Jon had escaped the bomb threat without injuring a human. Now he had to get to a phone and make that call.

Coleman stopped tugging at the bomb and plunged his hand into the desk drawer for a gun. The returning men would block the door soon, the only other exit from the room was a frosted-glass window that opened onto the mammoth bay of the warehouse.

Jon Venex plunged through the window in a welter of flying glass. The heavy thud of a recoilless .75 came from the room behind him and a foot-long section of metal window frame leaped outward. Another slug screamed by the robot's head as he scrambled toward the rear door of the warehouse.

He was a bare thirty feet away from the back entrance when the giant door hissed shut on silent rollers. All the doors would have closed at the same time, the thud of running feet indicated that they would be guarded as well. Jon hopped a section of packing cases and crouched out of sight.

He looked up over his head, there stretched a webbing of steel supports, crossing and recrossing until they joined the flat expanse of the roof. To human eyes the shadows there deepened into obscurity, but the infra-red from a network of steam pipes gave Jon all the illumination he needed.

The men would be quartering the floor of the warehouse soon, his only chance to escape recapture or death would be over their heads. Besides this, he was hampered by the loss of his leg. In the rafters he could use his arms for faster and easier travel.

Jon was just pulling himself up to one of the topmost crossbeams when a hoarse shout from below was followed by a stream of bullets. They tore through the thin roof, one slug clanged off the steel beam under his body. Waiting until three of the newcomers had started up a nearby ladder, Jon began to quietly work his way towards the back of the building.

Safe for the moment, he took stock of his position. The men were spread out through the building, it could only be a matter of time before they found him. The doors were all locked and — he had made a complete circuit of the building to be sure — there were no windows that he could force — the windows were bolted as well. If he could call the emergency operator the unknown friends of Venex 17 might come to his aid. This, however, was out of the question. The only phone in the building was on Coleman's desk. He had traced the leads to make sure.

His eyes went automatically to the cables above his head. Plastic gaskets were set in the wall of the building, through them came the power and phone lines. The phone line! That was all he needed to make a call.

With smooth, fast motions he reached up and scratched a section of wire bare. He laughed to himself as he slipped the little microphone out of his left ear. Now he was half deaf as well as half lame — he was literally giving himself to this cause. He would have to remember the pun to tell Alec Diger later, if there was a later. Alec had a profound weakness for puns.

Jon attached jumpers to the mike and connected them to the bare wire. A touch of the ammeter showed that no one was on the line. He waited a few moments to be sure he had a dial tone then sent the eleven carefully spaced pulses that would connect him with the local operator. He placed the mike close to his mouth.

"Hello, operator. Hello, operator. I cannot hear you so do not answer. Call the emergency operator — signal 14, I repeat — signal 14."

Jon kept repeating the message until the searching men began to approach his position. He left the mike connected — the men wouldn't notice it in the dark but the open line would give the unknown powers his exact location. Using his fingertips he did a careful traverse on an I-beam to an alcove in the farthest corner of the room. Escape was impossible, all he could do was stall for time.

"Mr. Coleman, I'm sorry I ran away." With the volume on full his voice rolled like thunder from the echoing walls.

He could see the men below twisting their heads vainly to find the source.

"If you let me come back and don't kill me I will do your work. I was afraid of the bomb, but now I am afraid of the guns." It sounded a little infantile, but he was pretty sure none of those present had any sound knowledge of robotic intelligence.

"Please let me come back . . . sir!" He had almost forgotten the last word, so he added another "Please, sir!" to make up.

Coleman needed that package under the boat very badly, he would promise anything to get it. Jon had no doubts as to his eventual fate, all he could hope to do was kill time in the hopes that the phone message would bring aid.

"Come on down, Junky, I won't be mad at you — if you follow directions." Jon could hear the hidden anger in his voice, the unspoken hatred for a robe who dared lay hands on him.

The descent wasn't difficult, but Jon did it slowly with much apparent discomfort. He hopped into the center of the floor — leaning on the cases as if for support. Coleman and Druce were both there as well as a group of hard-eyed newcomers. They raised their guns at his approach but Coleman stopped them with a gesture.

"This is *my* robe, boys, I'll see to it that he's happy."

He raised his gun and shot Jon's remaining leg off. Twisted around by the blast, Jon fell helplessly to the floor. He looked up into the smoking mouth of the .75.

"Very smart for a tin-can, but not smart enough. We'll get the junk on the boat some other way, some way that won't mean having you around under foot." Death looked out of his narrowed eyes.

Less than two minutes had passed since Jon's call. The watchers must have been keeping 24 hour stations waiting for Venex 17's phone message.

The main door went down with the sudden scream of torn steel. A whippet tank crunched over the wreck and covered the group with its multiple pom-poms. They were an instant too late, Coleman pulled the trigger.

Jon saw the tensing trigger finger and pushed hard against the floor. His head rolled clear but the bullet tore through his shoulder. Coleman didn't have a chance for a second shot, there was a fizzling hiss from the tank and the riot ports released a flood of tear gas. The stricken men never saw the gas-masked police that poured in from the street.

*J*on lay on the floor of the police station while a tech made temporary repairs on his leg and shoulder. Across the room Venex 17 was moving his new body with evident pleasure.

"Now this really feels like *something!* I was sure my time was up when that land slip caught me. But maybe I ought to start from the beginning." He stamped across the room and shook Jon's inoperable hand.

"The name is Wil Counter-4951L3, not that *that* means much anymore. I've worn so many different bodies that I forget what I originally looked like. I went right from factory-school to a police training school —

and I have been on the job ever since — Force of Detectives, Sergeant Jr. grade, Investigation Department. I spend most of my time selling candy bars or newspapers, or serving drinks in crumb joints. Gather information, make reports and keep tab on guys for other departments.

"This last job — and I'm sorry I had to use a Venex identity, I don't think I brought any dishonor to your family — I was on loan to the Customs department. Seems a ring was bringing uncut junk — heroin — into the country. F.B.I. tabbed all the operators here, but no one knew how the stuff got in. When Coleman, he's the local big-shot, called the agencies for an underwater robot, I was packed into a new body and sent running.

"I alerted the squad as soon as I started the tunnel, but the damned thing caved in on me before I found out what ship was doing the carrying. From there on you know what happened.

"Not knowing I was out of the game the squad sat tight and waited. The hop merchants saw a half million in snow sailing back to the old country so they had you dragged in as a replacement. You made the phone call and the cavalry rushed in at the last moment to save two robots from a rusty grave."

Jon, who had been trying vainly to get in a word, saw his chance as Wil Counter turned to admire the reflection of his new figure in a window.

"You shouldn't be telling me those things — about your police investigations and department operations. Isn't this information supposed to be secret? Specially from robots!"

"Of course it is!" was Wil's airy answer. "Captain Edgecombe — he's the head of my department — is an expert on all kinds of blackmail. I'm supposed to tell you so much confidential police business that you'll have to either join the department or be shot as a possible informer." His laughter wasn't shared by the bewildered Jon.

"Truthfully, Jon, we need you and can use you. Robes that can think fast and act fast aren't easy to find. After hearing about the tricks you pulled in that warehouse, the Captain swore to decapitate me permanently if I couldn't get you to join up. Do you need a job? Long hours, short pay — but guaranteed to never get boring."

Wil's voice was suddenly serious. "You saved my life, Jon — those snowbirds would have left me in that sandpile until all hell froze over. I'd like you for a mate, I think we could get along well together." The gay note came back into his voice, "And besides that, I may be able to save your life some day — I hate owing debts."

*T*he tech was finished, he snapped his tool box shut and left. Jon's shoulder motor was repaired now, he sat up. When they shook hands this time it was a firm clasp. The kind you know will last awhile.

Jon stayed in an empty cell that night. It was gigantic compared to the hotel and barrack rooms he was used to. He wished that he had his missing legs so he could take a little walk up and down the cell. He would have to wait until the morning. They were going to fix him up then before he started the new job.

He had recorded his testimony earlier and the impossible events of the past day kept whirling around in his head. He would think about it some other time, right now all he wanted to do was let his overworked circuits cool down, if he only had something to read, to focus his attention on. Then, with a start, he remembered the booklet. Everything had moved so fast that the earlier incident with the truck driver had slipped his mind completely.

He carefully worked it out from behind the generator shielding and opened the first page of *Robot Slaves in a World Economy.* A card slipped from between the pages and he read the short message on it.

PLEASE DESTROY THIS CARD AFTER READING
If you think there is truth in this book and would like to hear more, come to Room B, 107 George St. any Tuesday at 5 P.M.

The card flared briefly and was gone. But he knew that it wasn't only a perfect memory that would make him remember that message.